Tom and Ricky
and the
Lost Highrider

Bob Wright

High Noon Books

N

Cover Design: Nancy Peach
Interior Illustrations: Herb Heidinger

Glossary: factory, newspapers, machines, knob, channel, rig, CB radio, walkie-talkie, scanner

International Standard Book Number: 0-87879-392-5

10 09 08 07 06 05 04 03
15 14 13 12 11 10 9 8 7

You'll enjoy all the High Noon Books.
Write for a free full list of titles.

Contents

CHAPTER 1

A Missing Highrider

It was Friday. Tom and Ricky were on their way home from school. They were on their bikes. They turned on to Page Street.

"Look! There's Al Wilson," Tom said.

"That's funny. Al should be working today," Ricky said.

Al Wilson lived next door to Ricky. He was a good friend of Ricky's mom and dad.

"Maybe he's sick," Tom said.

"Hi, Al. What's up?" Ricky called out.

"I didn't go to work today," Al said.

"Are you sick?" Ricky said.

Both boys stopped their bikes. They walked over to Al. They liked Al. He helped them make things. He had lots of tools he let them use. He worked at the paper factory. He fixed all the machines there.

"What's going on, Al?" Ricky asked.

"My truck is gone," Al said.

Tom and Ricky looked up by Al's house. That's where he always parked it. Al's blue highrider wasn't there.

"Where is it?" Ricky asked.

"I don't know. I came out of the house this morning. But my highrider wasn't here," Al said.

"Can we help?" Tom asked.

"I don't think so," Al answered.

"Did you call Sergeant Collins?" Ricky asked.

"I sure did. I walked around looking for it. I thought it might be somewhere near here. But it wasn't. So I called him," Al said.

"What did he say?" Tom asked.

"He thinks it was stolen," Al answered.

"Does he have any ideas on who stole it?" Ricky asked.

"No. Not yet. But he said he would be on the lookout for it," Al said.

"Everyone in town knows your blue highrider. Someone will see it," Ricky said.

"That's what Sergeant Collins said, too," Al answered.

"How will you get to work at the paper factory tomorrow?" Tom asked.

"I don't know. They need me there. Those big paper machines always need to be fixed. I don't know who will do that work for me," Al said.

"I wish we could help you," Tom said.

"Talking about helping, we have to help Eddie," Ricky said.

"That's right. We have to go," Tom said.

"Where are you going?" Al asked.

"We're going to help Eddie with his newspapers," Ricky said.

4

"Newspapers?" Al asked.

"We're going to help Eddie get the newspapers to people. When we get done, we're going to see Eddie's new video game," Tom said.

"Let me or Sergeant Collins know if you see my blue highrider. Someone might be riding around in it," Al said.

"We sure will," Ricky said.

Tom and Ricky got on their bikes. They started off to meet Eddie on Front Street.

CHAPTER 2

Helping Eddie

Eddie was waiting for Tom and Ricky on Front Street. He had started to fold his newspapers.

"It's about time," he called out to them.

"Sorry, Eddie," Tom said.

"Well, come on. Let's get going," Eddie said.

Tom and Ricky got off their bikes. They started to help Eddie fold his newspapers.

"Did you hear the news?" Tom asked.

"What news?" Eddie asked.

"It's about Al Wilson," Tom said.

"Al Wilson? The man who lives next door to you, Ricky?" Eddie asked.

"That's the one. His highrider was stolen. We told him we'd be looking for it," Ricky said.

"Highrider? What's a highrider?" Eddie asked.

"Eddie, you know a lot about video games, but you don't know much about trucks," Tom said.

"OK, OK. So tell me," Eddie said.

"A highrider is like a truck. It's taller than other trucks. It has big tires. That way it can drive all over the place. It has a CB radio, too," Ricky said.

"What's the CB radio for?" Eddie asked.

"So he can talk to his friends. He can even talk to other people," Ricky answered.

"Highrider? What's a highrider?" Eddie asked.

"What else does it have?" Eddie asked.

"It has a good radio. I think it's the best rig in town," Ricky said.

"Does Al use it just to go to work?" Eddie asked.

"No. He uses it to go hunting," Ricky said.

"I think I'd like to have one some day," Eddie said.

"Me, too," Tom said.

"You know what?" Eddie asked.

"What's that?" Ricky said.

"Al is the only one who fixes the machines at the paper factory. If he can't get to work, there won't be any newspapers tomorrow," Eddie said.

"That's right," Tom said.

"Well, it looks like we're all done. Let's get the newspapers on our bikes," Eddie said.

"You take Front Street, Eddie. Tom, you can take Link Street. I'll take Page Street. We'll all meet at my house when we're done," Ricky said.

"OK. Then we can see if we can help Al," Tom said.

"Let's all look for Al's blue highrider," Eddie called out.

Then they all left.

CHAPTER 3

Back at Al's House

Ricky was the first one to get to Al's house. Tom got there next. Then Eddie got there.

"OK, we're all here. Now what do we do?" Tom asked.

"I think we could help Al by looking around. Maybe we'll find something," Ricky said.

"Like what?" Eddie asked.

"I don't know. We just might find something that would help Al," Ricky said.

"Where do you think Al is?" Tom asked.

"I don't know. Maybe he is with Sergeant Collins. Maybe they are looking around town for the blue highrider," Ricky answered.

"You two look around. I've got to go. I told Mr. West I'd be at the Video Store before it closed," Eddie said.

"OK. We'll let you know if we find anything," Ricky said.

Eddie got back on his bike. Then he left to go to the Video Store.

"Where do we start?" Tom asked.

"Let's go up to the house. That's where Al said he parked the truck," Ricky said.

They walked together up to the house.

All of a sudden Ricky called out, "Look at this."

"What is it?" Tom said.

"There's some glass on the ground. It's right where Al always parks his highrider," Ricky said.

"What's the big deal about glass?" Tom asked.

"You know Al. He would never leave anything around like that. He always keeps things neat," Ricky said.

"That's right. Al always takes care of his things," Tom said.

"I'm glad Patches isn't here. He would get cut on all that glass," Ricky said.

All of a sudden they heard a dog barking.

"Is that Patches?" Ricky asked.

Patches came running out from the bushes.

"He must have heard us talking," Tom said.

Patches kept on barking. He looked up at Ricky. Then he looked into the bushes. Then he looked back up at Tom and Ricky.

"It looks like he is trying to tell us something," Tom said.

"What is it, Patches?" Ricky asked.

Patches kept on barking.

"OK, OK. Come on, Tom. Let's see if there is something over there in those bushes," Ricky said.

They walked over to the bushes. Patches ran over and kept on barking.

"Tom. Look at this. Someone has been here," Ricky said.

"How do you know that?" Tom asked.

"Look at these bushes. They are all flat. It looks like someone has been standing in them," Ricky said.

"It sure does. Al always keeps his yard looking good. He wouldn't have done this," Tom said.

"That's right," Ricky said.

"Do you think this has anything to do with the lost highrider?" Tom asked.

"It might," Ricky answered.

"Well, let's keep on looking around," Tom said.

All of a sudden, Ricky said, "Wait. I think I found something. Look at this." He picked something off the ground.

"It looks like a knob," Ricky said.

"Let's see it," Tom said.

"It looks like a knob," Ricky said.

"A knob? Is that all?" Tom said.

"Anything might help. Even this knob might help Al find his highrider," Ricky said.

"But a knob has to go with something," Tom said.

"That's right. And look. It isn't dirty or old. That means it hasn't been here very long," Ricky said.

Patches started barking again. "Now what's wrong, Patches?" Ricky asked.

"I think I hear your mother calling you," Tom said.

"I have to go," Ricky said.

"I do, too," Tom said.

Ricky put the knob in his coat. "Call Eddie when you get home. Let's all meet here tomorrow morning."

"That's right. It will be Saturday. We can get started early to help Al," Tom said.

"Maybe we might find something else," Ricky said.

Tom left to go home. Ricky went next door to his house. Patches was right in back of him.

CHAPTER 4

Dusty Shows Up

Tom got to Ricky's house early on Saturday morning. Ricky was up and waiting for him.

"Come on in, Tom. Where's Eddie?" Ricky asked.

"I called him last night. He said he would be here," Tom said.

"You know Eddie. It's hard for him to get up out of bed," Ricky said.

"Do you have that knob?" Tom asked.

"I sure do," Ricky answered.

Ricky's dad walked into the room. "What are you two boys up to today?" he asked.

We're trying to help Al find his lost highrider," Ricky said.

"How are you going to do that?" Ricky's dad asked.

"We've been looking around. We found this by Al's house," Ricky said. He showed his father the knob.

"This knob had to come from somewhere. Al doesn't leave anything lying around. He takes care of things. That might be a help," his dad said.

"Ricky, I think we better go over and get Eddie. He might still be in bed," Tom said.

"We're going to go to Eddie's house," Ricky said to his dad.

"OK. Don't be gone too long. I'm going to work on the car," his dad said.

Ricky and Tom got on their bikes. Patches came running out of the house. "OK, Patches. You can come, too," Ricky said.

They went down Page Street and over to Front Street. It was still early. Most of the stores on Front Street were still closed.

"Look who I see," Tom said.

"It looks like Dusty," Ricky said.

It was Dusty. Dusty wasn't a friend of Tom and Ricky. Some people said he stole things. Not many people liked him.

"Ricky! Tom!" Dusty called out.

"What do you think he wants?" Tom asked.

"Let's find out," Ricky said.

They stopped their bikes by Dusty. Patches didn't like Dusty. He started to bark.

"Tell that dog to shut up," Dusty said.

"It's OK, Patches. Just sit," Ricky said.

"You're up early this morning," Tom said.

"Lots of people get up early," Dusty said.

Tom and Ricky looked at each other. They didn't like the way Dusty said that. Something was not right. But what?

"What's that in your hand?" Tom asked. He was looking at a black box.

"It's just a walkie-talkie," Dusty said.

"What do you have that for?" Tom asked.

Before Dusty could answer, Ricky said, "It's like a CB radio, only it's smaller."

"Can I look at it?" Ricky asked.

"That's right! You can carry it and you can talk to other people with it," Dusty said.

"Who do you talk to?" Tom asked.

"Oh, just some people I know," Dusty answered.

"Who?" Tom asked.

"You don't know them. Forget it," Dusty said.

"Can I look at it?" Ricky asked.

"You're already looking at it. I have to go. See you later," Dusty said. Then he started walking down Front Street.

"That was strange," Ricky said.

"You mean Dusty? Why? What's up? What are you thinking?" Tom asked.

"Dusty is the same as he always was. I mean his CB radio," Ricky answered.

"What about it?" Tom asked.

"One of the knobs was missing," Ricky said.

"Then that's why you wanted to get a good look at it," Tom said.

"That's right. Come on. Let's go over to Eddie's house," Ricky said.

They got back on their bikes. From Front Street they got onto Link Street. Patches was right in back of them.

CHAPTER 5

A Plan

Tom and Ricky rode down Link Street to Eddie's house. They got off their bikes and went up the front steps. Eddie opened the door.

"Where have you been?" Eddie asked.

"Where have we been? Where have you been?" Tom asked.

"I thought you said we'd all meet here," Eddie said.

"Oh, well. Forget it. We're here now," Ricky said.

"Did you find out anything new about Al's highrider?" Tom asked.

"Nothing. The only new thing is that old barn at the end of Link Street," Eddie said.

"What's that all about?" Ricky asked.

"Mr. Burns bought it. He's using it to fix up old trucks and old cars. He sure seems busy all the time," Eddie said.

"Did you get that new video game?" Tom asked.

"No. I got to the Video Store too late. It was closed. I'll go back today," Eddie said.

"We have a lot to tell you," Tom said.

"Have you found out anything about Al's missing highrider?" Eddie asked.

"No, not about the highrider. But we think we're on to something," Ricky said.

"What?" Eddie asked.

"We found this knob in the bushes at Al's house yesterday," Ricky said.

"A knob? What help is that?" Eddie asked.

"It's a new knob. It couldn't have been in the bushes very long," Ricky said.

"So what else is new?" Eddie asked.

"We saw Dusty up on Front Street this morning. He had a walkie-talkie. It was missing a knob," Ricky said.

"Ricky asked Dusty if he could look at the walkie-talkie, but Dusty wouldn't let him." Tom said.

"Do you think Dusty got the walkie-talkie from Al's highrider?" Eddie asked.

"We don't know yet," Ricky said.

"But Dusty can't drive a highrider," Eddie said.

"That's right. But there's something funny about all of this," Ricky said.

"And something else is funny," Tom said.

"What's that?" Eddie asked.

"We asked Dusty who he talked to on his walkie-talkie. He wouldn't tell us," Tom said.

"Looks kind of funny to me," Eddie said.

"It is funny," Ricky said.

"What do we do now?" Eddie asked.

"I have an idea," Ricky said.

"Let's hear it," Tom said.

"We know that anyone can use a CB or a walkie-talkie, right?" Ricky asked.

"Right," Tom said.

"And we want to know who Dusty talks to, right?" Ricky asked.

"Right, again," Tom said.

"So what do we do?" Ricky asked.

"We get some walkie-talkies," Tom yelled.

"Right again," Ricky said.

"Wait. Walkie-talkies? Where do we get them?" Tom asked.

"I know where," Eddie said.

"Where? Who would be selling things like walkie-talkies?" Tom asked.

"Mr. West sells them at his Video Store," Eddie said.

"That's right. We all have some money saved up," Ricky said.

"There's just one more thing," Tom said.

"What's that?" Eddie asked.

"We don't know how to use walkie-talkies," Tom said.

"We could ask Al Wilson. He knows a lot about walkie-talkies and CB radios," Ricky said.

"What about me? I know all about them. I'll show you how to use them," Eddie said.

"Well, let's get going," Ricky said.

They all ran out of Eddie's house. They were on their way to the Video Store.

CHAPTER 6

Getting Set Up

Tom, Ricky, and Eddie rode as fast as they could. They went down Link Street to Front Street. They stopped in front of Mr. West's Video Store.

"Can I help you boys?" Mr. West asked.

"You sure can," Eddie said.

"What do you need?" Mr. West asked.

"Do you have three walkie-talkies and a scanner?" Eddie asked.

"A scanner?" Tom said.

"I'll tell you about that later," Eddie said.

"I sure do. I have some that are used but they work very well," Mr. West said.

"We'll take them," Eddie said.

Mr. West went to get them.

"We're lucky. The used ones won't cost very much," Eddie said.

Mr. West came back with the three walkie-talkies and a scanner in a box. "Do you need anything else?" he asked.

"No. Not right now," Eddie said.

Tom, Ricky, and Eddie each got money and paid Mr. West. Then they ran out to their bikes.

"Come on. We have to get back to my house," Eddie said.

They got on their bikes. They got back to Eddie's house as fast as they could. Then they went to Eddie's room.

"OK. Let me tell you about these walkie-talkies," Eddie said.

"Start in. We're ready," Ricky said.

"Each walkie-talkie has two knobs. One knob turns it on and off. The same knob makes it loud or soft," Eddie said.

"What about the other knob?" Tom asked.

"The other knob lets you change channels," Eddie said.

"Just like a TV," Tom said.

"That's right," Eddie said.

"What about the scanner?" Ricky asked.

"The scanner saves you time. It moves from channel to channel all by itself. It stops when it hears people talking," Eddie said.

"Then we're all set," Ricky said.

"Wait. I'm mixed up. How are we going to use all of this?" Tom asked.

"We think Dusty might know something about Al's lost highrider. He might be using his walkie-talkie to talk to someone else," Ricky said.

"Should we tell Sergeant Collins?" Tom asked.

"We don't have much to go on. All we know is that we have a knob. Dusty's walkie-talkie is missing a knob," Ricky said.

"What will we do?" Tom asked.

"We will each take a walkie-talkie home. Tonight we will all wait to see if we hear Dusty," Eddie said.

"That's a good idea. We can call each other if we hear anything," Tom said.

Tom and Ricky each took a walkie-talkie. They left to go back home. They were going to be very busy that night.

CHAPTER 7

The Mystery is Solved

That night Tom, Ricky, and Eddie each had a walkie-talkie turned on. They were waiting to see if they could hear Dusty. It was getting late. Tom and Ricky fell asleep.

All of a sudden Ricky heard Eddie. Patches heard it, too. He started barking. Ricky jumped up out of bed.

"Break channel 6. Ricky! Ricky! Are you there?" Eddie said.

Ricky grabbed the walkie-talkie.

"I'm here, Eddie. What's up?" Ricky said.

"I just heard Dusty. He was on channel 8. Someone was telling him to stay behind some big cans at King's Market," Eddie said.

"I don't like this. I'm going to call Sergeant Collins," Ricky said.

All of a sudden Tom came in on the channel. "I heard what you said. What's going on?" he asked.

"We think Dusty is helping someone take things. It doesn't look good," Ricky said.

"Go ahead and call Sergeant Collins. Let us know what he says," Eddie said.

They all got off their walkie-talkies. Tom and Eddie waited.

Ricky called Sergeant Collins. He told him about the knob he found. Then he told him what Eddie heard on the walkie-talkie.

"Let me see that knob you found,"
Sergeant Collins said.

"Thanks for calling me, Ricky. I'll look into this right away. I'm going right now to King's Market. Why don't you, Tom, and Eddie come in and see me in the morning," the sergeant said.

"We sure will," Ricky said. Then Ricky called Tom and Eddie on channel 8.

The next morning the three boys went down to see Sergeant Collins.

"Let me see that knob you found," Sergeant Collins said.

Ricky gave him the knob.

Sergeant Collins took out a walkie-talkie that didn't have a knob. "Look. It fits," he said.

"That looks like the one Dusty had," Ricky said.

"It is the same one. I went down to King's Market last night. I found a man trying to take Mr. King's new truck. I found Dusty hiding in back of some big cans. I got them both," the Sergeant said.

"What did Dusty use his walkie-talkie for?" Tom asked.

"The man trying to take the truck had a walkie-talkie. That's how he and Dusty were able to take things," Sergeant Collins said.

Just then Al Wilson walked in.

"Al, look out the window," Sergeant Collins said.

Al looked out the window. "That's my highrider. I'd know it anywhere. But it's red."

"That's right. We found out last night that Dusty and his friend were taking cars and trucks to Mr. Burns on Link Street. Mr. Burns painted them and changed them. Then he sold them to a man in the next town," Sergeant Collins said.

"It was lucky that you boys found that knob. That really helped to solve this mystery," Al said.

"We were glad to help, Mr. Wilson," Ricky said.

"Some day when you are older I'm going to let you boys drive that highrider," Mr. Wilson said.

"We'd like that. We'd like that a lot," Tom said.

"And Eddie. Thanks for knowing a lot about walkie-talkies. That was another big help," Sergeant Collins said.

"And I'm going to pay for those walkie-talkies you had to buy," Al said.

"Come on, boys. Put your bikes in the back of the highrider. I'm going to give you a ride home. I'll show you what a highrider can really do," Al said.

"Oh, boy," Tom said.

"And I'm going to pay for those walkie-talkies you had to buy," Al said.

"Take care," Sergeant Collins called out.

Al, Tom, Ricky, and Eddie all ran out to the highrider for a ride they wouldn't forget.